Taliesin

The Boy Wizard

retold by Maggie Pearson

illustrated by David Wyatt

A & C Black • London

White Wolves Series Consultant: Sue Ellis,
Centre for Literacy in Primary Education

This book can be used in the White Wolves Guided Reading
programme with more experienced readers in Year 5.

First published 2004 by
A & C Black Publishers Ltd
37 Soho Square, London, W1D 3QZ

www.acblack.com

Text copyright © 2004 Maggie Pearson
Illustrations copyright © 2004 David Wyatt

The rights of Maggie Pearson and David Wyatt to be identified
as author and illustrator of this work respectively have been
asserted by them in accordance with the Copyrights, Designs
and Patents Act 1988.

ISBN 0-7136-6843-1

A CIP catalogue for this book is available
from the British Library.

A&C Black uses paper produced with elemental chlorine-free
pulp, harvested from managed sustained forests.

Printed and bound in Spain by G. Z. Printek, Bilbao.

Contents

For the seers, sages and storytellers of the future. Blessed be.

CHAPTER ONE
The Coming
of Taliesin

Long ago and far away, alone on an empty ocean under a sunless sky, a small leather bag bobbed up and down on the waves. Sometimes the bag gave a twitch, like a kick from something inside it. Sometimes it changed its lumpy shape into a different shape entirely (but still just as lumpy) – as if that something inside was making itself more comfortable.

Now and again came the echo of a sound that was neither quite the shushing of the waves nor yet

the whispering of the wind, though there was something in it of both. It was as if the bag was quietly singing to itself.

Time passed. Wind and waves and tide carried the little bag shorewards towards a river's mouth where a man sat fishing.

It wasn't that the man liked fishing. Nor was he a fisherman by trade. He was Elphin, cousin to the King and lord of all the lands around, though you'd never have known it to look at him. His clothes were patched, his hair looked as if he'd fallen through a hedge and the horse cropping the grass beside him was the sorriest-looking creature that ever went on four legs.

Lord Elphin was the unluckiest man in the whole of Wales. The sort who never gets asked on picnics, because if he goes along it's bound to rain. What was worse, his bad luck seemed to be catching. There hadn't been one good harvest since his father's time.

Then someone had a bright idea.

It was said that if a fisherman set his nets across the river's mouth on May Day Eve he was bound to have good luck. There was talk of men who'd caught a hundred pounds' worth of fish – brought to them by the incoming tide, without them lifting a finger! – all in that one night.

"I'm not a fisherman," protested Elphin. "I'm cousin to the King!" Though he had to admit a hundred pounds would come in handy for fixing the castle roof.

The fishermen weren't too keen on the idea either; they didn't want Elphin the Unlucky spoiling the luck of the weir, though none of them was in any hurry to try it for himself. They'd got better things to do on May Eve. Things like feasting and dancing and keeping the bonfires blazing bright to scare off the witches and hobgoblins.

There was way too much magic about on that night of the year for any sane man to want to sit by himself on a damp

10

riverbank in the dark.

"Witches?" scoffed Elphin. "Poppycock! As for hobgoblins – I wouldn't know one if I saw one. Would you?"

That settled it. They took him down to the rivermouth and showed him how to set his nets.

"Now all you have to do," they said, "is wait till morning."

There they left him.

So there he sat, through the long, cold hours of darkness. Every time the moon peeped out from behind the clouds (which wasn't often) it gave Elphin just enough light to see that his nets were still empty. Not a ripple; not a splash; not one shimmer of a single silvery fish.

Unless—

What was that, bobbing on the incoming tide? Something darker and more solid than the foam-flecked water carrying it bob-bob-bobbing towards the weir, then – bob-bob – back again. It wasn't a fish; too dark. Nor a piece of driftwood; too round! But lumpy with it. Elphin screwed up his eyes to see better.

Then the clouds covered the moon again. And the sea-mist came rolling in with the tide; a clinging mist that coiled long cold fingers around him, chilling him to the bone.

Elphin wrapped his cloak tighter and pulled his feet up under it, but he was still shivering. He thought of the feasting and dancing going on back in the village.

Oh, to be sitting now beside a roaring bonfire, tucking into a potato baked in its embers and topped with lashings of butter! And something warming to drink! But if he listened carefully he could just hear the odd snatch of music – there it came again! A sweet voice singing. He could even make out the words:

"Sigh no more, Elphin.

Cry no more, Elphin ..."

They hadn't quite forgotten him after all.

"Sigh no more ..."

The unearthly melody dipped and soared like the ebb and flow

of the waves.

"Cry no more ..."

Perhaps there was some special magic in the air that night; it sounded to Elphin as if his mother's voice was singing to him; singing him back to sleep when he was very little, after he'd woken from a bad dream. As if all his troubles until now had been nothing but one long bad dream.

Morning came, a bright, cold May Day morning with a scent of blossom in the air. Elphin woke and stretched, feeling strangely happy; perhaps after all this was going to be his lucky day.

He strolled down to the water's edge and began pulling in his nets.

Not one fish did he find – so, no surprises there; he was still Elphin the Unlucky – but only an old leather bag.

Perhaps my hundred pounds is in it, thought Elphin, still willing to look on the bright side. All in gold pieces. That would be most fitting for the cousin to the King!

Then the bag gave a kick. There was something alive inside. Perhaps it's a puppy, thought Elphin. A poor little mongrel puppy that somebody tried to drown. He'd always wanted a dog. Or it might be a litter of kittens.

Elphin listened, but no sound came from inside the leather bag. Perhaps he was already too

15

late. That would be terrible. He fumbled with the knots. At last he pulled the bag open.

Out popped – not a puppy; nor a kitten – but a baby! A baby with golden curls and skin so white it dazzled the eyes to look at him.

"Oh, Taliesin!" Elphin exclaimed.

(Luckily, being a Welshman, Elphin had spoken in Welsh. In English the words would have come out as something like, "What a bright face!" Which isn't the sort of name any boy wants to be saddled with.)

"Taliesin," repeated the baby. "Yes, Taliesin will do very nicely. I was wondering when someone would get round to giving me a name."

Elphin was so surprised to hear the baby speak, he nearly dropped it.

"So little and already talking!"

"Oh, I can talk and I can sing too," said Taliesin. "Sigh no more, Elphin. Sigh no more; you've caught yourself the son you always longed for. Isn't that a whole lot better than a hundred pounds' worth of wet fish?"

"A son?" echoed Elphin. "How did you know I always wanted a son? How did you know my name?"

"I may be small, but my knowledge is great. I'm only just beginning to discover the half of

it myself. But, wise as I am, I cannot go wandering through the world at my age. So wrap me up in your cloak before we both catch our death of cold and carry me home to your lovely wife, Olwen."

"You know about Olwen too?"

"I know that though you're poor and shabby and the unluckiest man in all Wales, Olwen loves you."

That was true; the one good thing in Elphin's unlucky life was Olwen.

What was Olwen going to say? Not only had he failed to catch so much as a single fish for their dinner, he was bringing home—

"A baby!" cried Olwen, taking Taliesin in her arms. "Isn't that just what we've always wanted? Didn't they say the weir always brings good luck? And he's beautiful."

"So are you," said Taliesin, beaming up at her. "I knew you would be."

"I forgot to warn you," said Elphin. "He talks."

"So he does! Who's a clever boy, then? But how did you come to be in that old leather bag?"

"It's a long story," said Taliesin. "Right now I need—"

"A bath!" said Olwen, wrinkling her nose.

There's nothing like a new baby for turning a household

upside down. There's a room to be turned into a nursery; a cot to be found and a nursemaid; baby clothes and nappies ...

"A baby!"

"A new baby!"

"Tossed up by the sea?"

"True as I'm standing here. Ask Lord Elphin; he'll show you the bag to prove it."

"Poor old Elphin! Another mouth to feed."

"Lucky for the baby, though; if Elphin hadn't been there ..."

"Can I hold him for a minute?"

"Let me! Oh, cootchy-cootchy-coo!"

Taliesin let himself be passed around like a game of pass-the-parcel and never spoke a word till he was alone again with Elphin and Olwen.

"Evening is the best time for stories," said Taliesin. "Evening and firelight and the shadows lengthening."

For a while they sat in silence, save for the crackling of the fire. Then the flames began to flicker and sway, as if stirred by a mountain breeze.

Elphin looked round to see if the door was open; but no.

"I can smell pine trees," whispered Olwen. "And wild thyme."

Higher the flames danced, and higher, casting long shadows on the walls, till the walls lost

their smoothness and the stones flowed into one another, turning back into the rough rock they were hewn from.

They seemed to be all three sitting in a cave on a wild mountainside and on the fire now sat a bubbling cauldron.

Elphin wrinkled his nose: "Something's burning."

"It's beginning, isn't it? Your story," whispered Olwen. "I can see her – oh! She's angry!"

"Who is she?" whispered Elphin.

"Caridwen," said Taliesin. "A powerful witch – but nowhere near as powerful as she wanted to be. This is her story – and mine. It's called …"

22

CHAPTER TWO
The Witch's Brew

"Curses!" screamed the witch, Caridwen. She kicked the cauldron, stubbed her toe and yelled "Curses!" again.

You might think she was overreacting (said Taliesin) about a bit of stew that got burnt, but this was no ordinary brew. Whoever drank this brew would gain the knowledge of all things that were and are and shall be, plus a whole lot more besides. Caridwen wasn't interested in the details. All she knew was that this

25

spell would turn her into the most powerful witch that ever was.

But it's one thing to have the recipe for such strong magic and quite another to cook it. The cauldron had to simmer for a year and a day. And certain ingredients must only be added at their proper time and season. Things like hemlock dug in the dark, mandrake root, or dead men's fingers aren't always easy to come by when you need them – not fresh anyway.

Time and again Caridwen came home triumphant after long searching to find the precious brew had burned or boiled over or that she'd simply run out of firewood.

Still muttering curses,

26

Caridwen lugged the cauldron outside and began pouring the stuff away again.

"Wait! Dear lady, wait!"

Who was that? Calling to her on that lonely mountainside? (Calling her a lady, too!)

It was an old blind man called Morda. And before you ask me (said Taliesin) how a blind man knew what Caridwen was doing, I'll tell you. It was because he had a boy with him, tethered to a piece of string, whose job it was to lead him about and tell him everything that was going on.

The boy's name was Gwion. (And don't ask me how the blind man and his boy came to be

passing that way. Just call it fate.)

"Dear lady!" puffed Morda. The path was steep and hard to climb. "Dear lady, don't throw good food away. Here are two hungry mouths that would thank you for a bite to eat."

"You wouldn't," said Caridwen, "not if I gave you this to eat, because the two of you would be stone dead. This stuff is poison." Then she had an idea. "I will feed you both," she said. "And I'll give you a home for a year and a day. But you'll have to work for it, mind."

She scoured out the pot, put a fresh brew on to boil and set Gwion to stirring it while Morda stoked the fire.

Morda was happy enough. He'd got a roof over his head and three meals a day. But Gwion was a boy and boys get bored. Boys get curious when they're given a job to do and not told why. Stirring a foul-smelling cauldron day after day after day ...

"What's it for, anyway?" demanded Gwion, peering into the cauldron for the umpteenth time.

"Witch's business," said Morda. "Just keep stirring."

Gwion sighed. "How long have we been here?"

"A year and a day come lunchtime, by my reckoning. What day are we today? If it's Thursday,

that means chicken."

"A year and a day! That's one tenth of my life!"

"Sh! She'll hear you."

Caridwen was resting at the back of the cave, waiting for the moment when she'd taste that brew and feel all the knowledge and the power and the magic of it flowing through her.

"How much longer do we have to stay?" Gwion was stirring furiously now.

Maybe it was just a boy's carelessness. On the other hand, maybe that brew, being so full of magic, didn't want to be wasted on Caridwen. Three drops of liquid flew out of the cauldron and settled on Gwion's finger. Three precious drops! That was all it took.

"Ow!" cried Gwion, dropping the spoon so he could suck his finger.

Then "Oh!" he cried, as the knowledge of all that was and is and shall be came crowding into his head.

"What is it?" cried Morda.

"Oh, Morda, I would tell you, if I had the time. I would tell you everything – from the beginning of the world to its very end – oh! and make a song about it too! But Caridwen will have the skin from my back and the head from my shoulders if I don't make a run for it now! Goodbye, Morda!"

Gwion was off! Out of the

cave and down the mountainside. The rest of the brew boiled up and cracked the cauldron clean in two with an almighty CLANG! fit to wake the dead. Caridwen came running just in time to see her year's work sink, bubbling, into the floor.

She shrieked. She cursed. She howled.

"Dear lady," cried Morda, "don't blame me. Whatever the matter is, it was the boy's fault."

"Of course it was," said Caridwen. "Boys are always trouble." She tucked up her skirts and ran on the wings of the wind after the boy Gwion.

Oh my! thought Gwion when he saw her coming, I would need

to be a hare to outrun her.

At that, some bit of the new knowledge that was in his head must have come into play. At once Gwion became a hare, bounding through the long grass.

But Caridwen, being a witch, already knew a trick worth two of that.

Next time Gwion snatched a glance behind him, it was not Caridwen but a greyhound that was chasing him – and gaining fast!

And ahead of him now lay a river.

The greyhound behind you and the wide river ahead! What would you do? Gwion chose the river, leaping high into the air, trusting to the knowledge in his

head to do the rest.

Before he hit the water, he'd changed from a hare to a fish, which is a wonderful, magical thing to be, gliding in and out among the reeds – if there is not an otter on your tail, with a look of Caridwen about it!

Are you still there? thought Gwion. Well, then, I'll be a bird. He kicked with his tail towards the surface. Up, up he soared, out of the blue-green water, into the blue, blue sky.

But this shape-shifting magic is not so easily done. It was a poor little fledgling bird he became, scarcely fit to be out of the nest.

And Caridwen was a hawk,

soaring high above him, scanning the air below her, till she found him. Down she plunged for the kill, talons at the ready.

Gwion dropped before her like a stone – there was no other way to go. Below him he saw a threshing floor on which lay thousands upon thousands of grains of corn.

The very thing! How could Caridwen ever find the one grain of corn that was Gwion among so many?

But Caridwen was not a quitter. In the form of a little black hen she *scritch-scritch-scratched* among those grains of corn, turning them over one by one, until she felt one twitch with fear in

her beak. (Gwion was still only human after all.) She tossed back her head and swallowed him down.

"And that," said Caridwen, "is the end of that!"

But it wasn't. Not by a long way.

★ ★ ★

In time Caridwen gave birth to a baby. The minute she saw him she knew that wrapped up inside him was all the power and knowledge Gwion had stolen from her. Her first thought was to kill him. Oh, but he was so, so beautiful, with his head of golden curls and his white, shining face.

Then again, maybe she was afraid of where that powerful

magic might turn up next if she did kill him. So she put him in a leather bag and threw him into the sea.

"If it is his fate to live," she said, "why, then he'll live. And if he dies it will be the sea's doing, not mine."

"And here I am!" cried Taliesin. "Carried to you by the wind and waves. It was fate that brought me to you, Elphin. Your fate and mine."

Elphin said nothing. He was still dizzy from the story of the chase. He'd felt himself running with the hare – swimming like a fish – soaring like a bird – and was staring down Caridwen's moist, red throat, thinking his

last hour had come when he'd found himself with a jolt back by his own fireside.

Olwen chuckled: "A baby, from a grain of corn? I don't believe it!"

"That's my story," grinned Taliesin. "And I'm sticking to it. Now, if you don't mind – I think I need changing again."

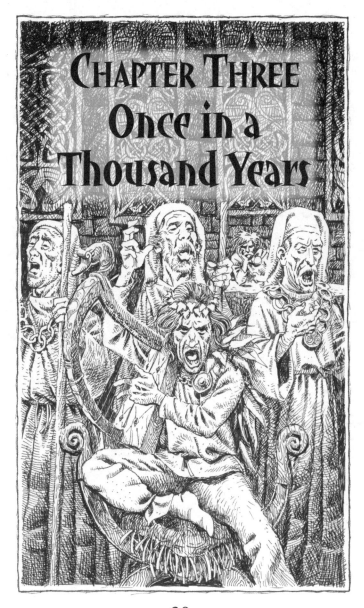

CHAPTER THREE
Once in a Thousand Years

Twelve years it takes in the ordinary way of things to train a druid and a bard. Twelve years of hard study. Not to mention the cold baths and the sitting in pitch-dark rooms waiting for inspiration.

But once in a thousand years, if the world is lucky, there comes one who has it all, already in his head, from the moment he is born.

Such a one was Taliesin.

So he spent his twelve years with Elphin and Olwen

practising what he already knew. Soon it was whispered that Elphin must have caught the magic salmon of wisdom in that net of his. To know so much! To have such power! And to give such good advice!

Suddenly, Elphin seemed to know how to heal the sick; and how to make sure there was rain to make the crops grow and sunshine for the harvest. He would give advice to anyone who asked for it; whether this one should marry that; whether a merchant should send his ship north, south, east or west, and when it should set sail to avoid the storms; whether a farmer should sow wheat or turnips. And his advice was always good.

Nobody gave a thought to the baby in the cradle at his side. Except maybe to think what a devoted father he was when he bent down to tickle the baby's toes – "Go on," he'd say; "I'm listening."

Nobody looked twice at the child playing at Elphin's feet, unless Elphin turned away for a moment to admire some treasure the toddler had found.

By the time Taliesin was twelve years old they'd grown so used to the boy who was always by Elphin's side and, now and then, whispered in his ear, it was almost as if Taliesin had learned how to make himself invisible.

In the evenings, alone with

Elphin and Olwen, Taliesin would tell them stories, sing them songs – of Noah's Ark or the ten years' war of Troy – weaving pictures out of the empty air as he had on that first, magical evening.

He told them the tale of Gwydion, the magician who made a woman out of flowers, filling the air with the scents of meadowsweet and oak and broom.

He told them of the Children of Lir, changed by their wicked stepmother into swans and doomed for three times three hundred years to wander the lonely seas. And Elphin and Olwen felt the salt spray on their faces, tasted it on their tongues and listened to the sad, sweet song of the swans.

Life was good. For everyone.

Then, when Taliesin was twelve years old, Elphin was invited to the King's court for Christmas.

It was a thing that had never happened before, though Elphin was the King's own cousin. King Maelgwyn had a lot of cousins and no time for his poor relations. Now Maelgwyn had heard that Elphin's luck had taken a turn for the better.

"I can't go," said Elphin. "I won't go. I'd much rather stay at home for Christmas."

"You must go," said Olwen. "The King commands it."

"Then you must come too."

But the invitation was only

45

for one.

"I won't know what to do or what to say!"

"The main thing to remember," said Taliesin, "is that King Maelgwyn is the wisest and most generous man who ever walked the Earth. His wife is the most beautiful, his horses run the fastest, his army is the strongest, and his kingdom the happiest."

"Really?" said Elphin.

"No, not really. Just keep saying it anyway."

"So King Maelgwyn is the wisest and most beautiful and his wife runs the fastest ... No, that can't be right!" Elphin was hopeless at telling lies.

"Don't worry about it," said

46

Taliesin. "There will be plenty of people there to remind you."

So off went Elphin, the King's own cousin, to take his rightful place at the King's court for Christmas. And found himself hating every minute of it.

Every day was one long round of hunting and jousting, music and dancing and party games, acrobats and rope-dancers and jugglers and performing animals. It made his poor head ache.

He had been looking forward to hearing the King's bards sing, which he was told they did every evening after dinner – all twenty-four of them. A good bard was supposed to have the power to

47

make men laugh; or make them weep; or make them sleep.

What a disappointment!

First the bards third-class marched into the hall, noses in the air, dressed in white robes and carrying wands made of bronze.

Next came the bards of the second grade, two by two, pointing their noses even higher, as if one of them had made a rude smell, but the rest were too polite to mention it. They, too, were dressed in white, but their wands were all of silver.

After them strutted the bards of the first grade, also in white, but with wands of solid gold. If they'd tried to point their noses any higher, they'd have fallen over backwards.

All the wands were hung with little bells.

The tinkling of the bells stopped conversation dead. Servants clearing away the dishes froze like statues. Even the dogs fighting for scraps under the tables knew something was up. The hall was still and silent as the King's chief bard, Heinin Vardd, wearing his ceremonial feathered cloak of many colours, made his entrance. He strode to the front of the hall.

The bards lined up behind him. Heinin Vardd gave them the note to begin on and the bards began to sing.

49

The song they sang was always pretty much the same.

They'd begin by praising the King. Then they'd go on to praise the Queen. After that they praised the King's horses and all his men. They praised the King's wealth and wisdom and generosity – especially his generosity, hoping he'd give them all nice, fat Christmas presents. A little something in gold, perhaps?

Elphin would yawn and sigh, longing for home. To sit with his feet up by his own fireside, with Olwen bringing in the mince pies and Taliesin telling the story of the first Christmas. And by the fire's light he'd see the baby in the manger, the ox and the ass kneeling, the shepherds and the wise men from the East who'd followed a bright star across mountains and deserts ...

It was not long before someone asked him why he looked so glum.

Like a fool, Elphin told him.

It was not long after that before someone told the King. Maelgwyn liked to have people around him who told tales. It kept the rest of the court in order.

"Elphin says he doesn't like it here, Your Majesty," whispered one crony.

"He says he'd rather be at home," smirked another.

"He says his bard is better than all twenty-four of yours put

together."

"He says his wife is more beautiful—"

"Stop!" roared the King.

"Is this true?" he asked Elphin.

Elphin could have saved himself with a thumping great flattering lie. But Elphin had been brought up to tell the truth. Besides, Elphin had had enough of court life to last him a lifetime.

"It's true," he said. "I'm sorry. Can I go home now, please?"

"Throw him in the dungeon!" roared the King. "Chain him up! And throw away the key."

Someone, braver than the rest, reminded Maelgwyn that Elphin was his cousin, a prince of the royal blood.

"Better make the chains of silver then," said Maelgwyn. "Eh? Eh?"

It was a joke. Everyone laughed – except poor Elphin.

Alone in his bare prison cell, Elphin closed his eyes. "Oh, Taliesin," he sighed, "why didn't you warn me? Why did you let me come?"

He was only a little surprised to hear Taliesin answer from somewhere inside his head: "Think about it; things could have been a lot worse if you'd refused the King's invitation."

Taliesin chuckled: "Look on the bright side; at least you don't have to listen to those bards

droning on any more."

"What will happen now?"

"Don't worry; I'll get you out of there. For the moment, you must wait. My place is here, with Olwen."

"What's the matter? Is she in trouble?" Elphin opened his eyes and looked about him. He was alone in the cell. Of course he was.

As soon as he closed his eyes again, he heard Taliesin answer; "Nothing I can't handle. And I will come for you. Sleep now. Sweet dreams."

Elphin settled down to sleep. And he did have sweet dreams.

★ ★ ★

"What's wrong, Taliesin?" demanded Olwen. "You had a

faraway look in your eyes; your lips were moving but I couldn't hear the words. Is Elphin all right?"

"He's well," said Taliesin. "Maelgwyn's keeping him safe until we go to fetch him home again."

"Then let's go now."

"Not yet; we have a visitor to entertain."

"A visitor?"

"He'll be here by evening."

"Who?"

"The King's son – Rhun."

"Rhun!" She'd heard of Rhun – everyone had heard of Rhun; Rhun was a bully whose chief fun in life was making it miserable for other people; creating

mischief, telling lies.

Rhun was curious to see this wonderful wife of Elphin's for himself. Now he was on his way, his head spinning with mischief-making schemes.

"I won't have that dreadful man in my house!" cried Olwen.

"You can't shut him out," said Taliesin. "He is the King's son, after all. So let's ask him in. We'll treat him as he deserves. Trust me."

Then he sent her to put on her plainest dress while he went downstairs to the kitchen.

"Come with me," he said to the scullery maid whose job it was to gut the fish for dinner.

She followed Taliesin up the

stairs, wiping her hands on her apron and trying to pick the bits of dough from under her fingernails, where she'd been kneading bread that afternoon.

"Take your pick from my lady's wardrobe," Taliesin told her. "Just for tonight you shall be the lady and my lady shall wait on you. Hurry now, the King's son is almost at the door!"

The kitchen maid didn't need telling twice. She picked out the richest clothes she could find, never mind whether they matched one another or not, or whether she could get them done up. With pins and extra laces and careful draping of shawls and a lot of breathing in, she made them fit.

After all, she wasn't likely to get the chance again. Then she chose the biggest earrings, the heaviest necklaces and half a dozen bracelets. Such a pity there wasn't a ring to fit her fat little fingers; but here was Elphin's own signet ring! Well, Taliesin had told her to help herself. She jammed it on her little finger. She was ready to meet the King's son, Rhun.

It was the strangest sight that met Rhun when he came knocking at the door. He never noticed the girl in the plain brown dress that opened it. His eyes were on the walking Christmas tree with hands outstretched to greet him.

So this is Elphin's wonderful

wife! sneered Rhun to himself.

If he'd spared a glance for the same girl in the plain brown dress who served them dinner, he might have wondered whether she might not be the real lady and the other one the maid.

Rhun was too busy working out the story he'd tell when he got back to court.

How they'd laugh when they heard about Elphin's fat, red-faced wife, who drank her soup straight out of the bowl instead of using a spoon; who wiped her greasy fingers on the tablecloth; who laughed so loudly at his jokes that his ears were still ringing with the sound; who drank enough beer to float a medium-sized boat;

and finally collapsed across the table fast asleep and snoring! Elphin wouldn't be able to deny it – not when Rhun produced that tell-tale signet ring he'd noticed on her little finger.

He tugged at it – the kitchen maid snored on – but the ring wouldn't come off.

Rhun was not the sort of man to let a little thing like that stop him. He took out his dagger and chopped off the finger, ring and all before Olwen could stop him. The kitchen maid opened her eyes, looked up at him and giggled, then settled to sleep again.

Off went Rhun, back to his father's castle.

"How could you let him do

that?" Olwen cried to Taliesin.

"Sh!"

The kitchen maid snored on and never felt a thing.

"Let be what will be," said Taliesin. "This will be her only proof that she didn't dream it all." He took the girl's hand, rubbed cobwebs on it, whispered some words and healed it so well that it was days before she counted up her fingers and found that she really was one short.

She didn't mind. Just for one night she'd been like Cinderella, dining with the King's own son. One day, perhaps, he'd come back and marry her. Meanwhile, it was back to the kitchen and the fish.

* * *

Back at court, Elphin was brought up from the dungeons in his silver chains to hear Rhun tell the court all about his fat, vulgar, drunken wife.

Elphin knew it wasn't true. But everyone else thought it was – or at least, might be – and though some of them felt sorry for Elphin, they sniggered and laughed when the King did, or shook their heads and looked disapproving: such behaviour for a lady! It was hard to believe.

This was Rhun's big moment.

"And if you don't believe me," he said, "here is Elphin's ring, still on the finger that wore it!"

Ugh! Elphin shut his eyes tight.

"Look at it!" roared Maelgwyn. "Is that your ring?"

Elphin couldn't bring himself to look. "Oh, Taliesin!" he whispered. "How could you have let it happen?"

Somewhere inside his head he heard Taliesin's voice: "Your ring on Olwen's finger? Think about it, Elphin! Then open your eyes and look. Look hard at the finger, not the ring; and think before you speak."

Elphin thought about it. He opened his eyes and looked.

Then he began to laugh.

"That is my ring," he said. "But it was never on my wife's finger. It's much too big. She could never put it on her thumb without it sliding off again. Look

63

at that dough under the fingernail! Do you think my wife makes her own bread? Do you think my wife doesn't trim her nails every Saturday night without fail? This nail has not been trimmed for a month or more! And from the faint smell of fish, I would say at a guess, Rhun, that you have been having dinner with my kitchen maid!"

Then everyone began laughing at Rhun, who couldn't tell a lady from a kitchen maid. It was the best joke they'd heard all Christmas.

Rhun was a bad loser.

Elphin found himself back in the dungeon again and this time Rhun saw to it that they really did throw away the key.

CHAPTER FOUR
The Battle of the Bards

"In prison?" said Olwen. "What's Elphin doing in prison? How long has he been there? And why you didn't tell me?"

"Don't worry," said Taliesin. "We're going to get him out."

"If you've got another clever plan, I don't want to hear it. This time I'll deal with things myself."

"I knew you'd say that," said Taliesin. "I've got the horses saddled and waiting."

The two of them arrived at court just as the King was sitting

down to dinner. Never mind that! Olwen marched up to him, curtsied (after all, he was the King), then stood up straight and looked him in the eye.

"I am Lord Elphin's wife," she said. "I have come to fetch my husband home. Now!"

"Er," said the King. He wasn't used to people being firm with him. "I see Elphin told the truth about you," he said. "You are a lot prettier than the Queen." She'd still got all her fingers too, he noticed. He glanced at Rhun. Rhun was staring at her with a haven't-I-seen-you-somewhere-before look on his face.

"Elphin always tells the truth, poor, silly man," she said. "You shouldn't lock a man up for telling the truth."

"Sit down," said Maelgwyn soothingly. "Have a bite to eat. You must be tired after your journey. Afterwards we'll sort things out."

Olwen sat down at the King's high table.

Taliesin found himself a place at the far end of the hall, among the squires and younger sons.

After dinner it was time for the bards to perform as usual.

First the bards of the third class made their entrance, noses in the air, wands of bronze in their hands.

As they passed him, Taliesin put his fingers to his lips and

made a very rude noise that is hard to spell. If you had to write it, it would be something like *Blerwm, blerwm.*

The bards were outraged, but they couldn't so much as glance his way. It would not have been dignified.

"*Blerwm, blerwm,*" went Taliesin, as the second-grade bards passed by, with the bells tinkling on their wands of silver.

"*Blerwm, blerwm,*" as the bards of the first grade entered, striking their golden wands on the ground as they came.

Then Heinin Vardd made his entrance, splendid in his cloak of many-coloured feathers. He was surprised to find the hall not so quiet as usual. Some people at the back were even giggling.

Somewhere a small voice was going, *"Blerwm, blerwm."*

Heinin Vardd pretended he hadn't heard it. But he saw the boy that made the noise – oh, yes! He saw him.

The bards took their places before the King's high table. They lifted up their heads, waiting for Heinin Vardd to give them the signal to begin. The Chief Bard raised his fingers to his lips. *"Blerwm, blerwm!"*

"Blerwm, blerwm!" chorussed the rest of the bards.

Heinin Vardd turned round and glared. The rest shuffled their feet and looked at one another

71

sideways, then back at Heinin Vardd, as if to say, "Don't blame *me*; he started it!" They waited for Heinin Vardd to start them off again. Heinin Vardd took a deep breath.

"*Blerwm, blerwm!*" went Heinin Vardd, looking as dignified as he knew how.

"*Blerwm, blerwm!*" echoed the rest. This time they carried on: "*Blerwm, blerwm! Blerwm, blerwm! Blerwm, blerwm, blerwm!*"

The guests looked at one another; was it a joke?

Not a very good one, judging from the look on Maelgwyn's face.

"What is the meaning of this?" he roared.

There seemed to be no way of stopping them – "*Blerwm, blerwm!*

Blerwm, blerwm!" – till Rhun cuffed the chief bard round the head so hard that he fell over. That broke the spell.

Heinin Vardd picked himself up and glared at Rhun.

"Well?" the King demanded.

"Don't blame me, your majesty," said Heinin Vardd. "We are bewitched. There is a devil in the hall in the shape of that boy!"

The chief bard swung round to point an accusing finger only to find Taliesin already beside him.

"Who are you?" demanded Maelgwyn.

"I am Lord Elphin's bard," said Taliesin.

"A boy?" scoffed Rhun. "I suppose you're the best that Elphin

can afford."

"I am the best," said Taliesin.

Heinin Vardd drew himself up. "What right have you to call yourself a *blerwm-blerwm*-bard? The making of a *blerwm*-bard takes twelve years of hard study."

"Twice twelve bards may study for twice twelve years," said Taliesin, "and still find no better song between them than *blerwm-blerwm*. This body of mine is young but the knowledge that is in it is older than the making of the world." Nobody could be sure at what moment Taliesin began to sing, but sing he did:

> *"For I was there when the world was born, out of the darkness and into the light …"*

"I was there at the building of the Ark.

"I was in the rain that fell for forty days and forty nights. I was in the flight of the raven and the dove ..."

It was as if the song had always been there, waiting to be given a voice. The music of a dance begun at the first moment of creation, in which all creatures of the Earth and above the Earth and under the sea, the rocks, the trees, the waters and the stars joined hands and moved in shifting patterns till the end of time ...

I am earth!
I am water!
I am air!
I am fire!

*I have been a stag, running
   free upon the mountain.
I have ridden on the dolphin's
   back,
to the kingdoms under the sea...*
On and on he sang:
*I was little Gwion.
For a while yet
   my fate is to be Taliesin.
But my true home is somewhere
   among the stars.*

There was silence in the hall.
But somewhere, it seemed, the
song continued, unheard by
mortal ears.

Maelgwyn said shakily,
"That was a good song. A very
good song. Name your reward!"

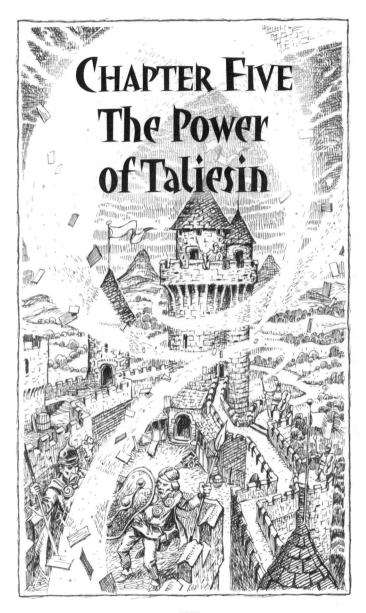

CHAPTER FIVE
The Power
of Taliesin

It was the custom in those days for a bard to ask anything he liked in payment for a really good song. A horse, maybe. A warm cloak for the winter. A gold chain to wear. Most bards knew roughly what they were worth and knew better than to ask too much.

Most princes knew better than to refuse them.

So, "Name your reward!" said Maelgwyn.

"Set Lord Elphin free," said Taliesin.

"Choose something else," said Maelgwyn.

Taliesin shook his head. "There's nothing else I want."

"Then the answer is no."

"You'll change your mind," said Taliesin.

"What will you do to make me change it?" sneered Maelgwyn. "Make up a rude song about me and sing it wherever you go?"

It was said that a good bard, if he was really angry, could make up a song that would bring the subject out in spots and boils. Nobody had actually seen it done, but it was bad enough to have a bard singing a rude song about you wherever he went. A king has his pride. It's not very nice to know that all the people in all the kingdoms round about think you're a bit of a joke.

"I am a seer as well as a bard," said Taliesin. "And I tell you that before another hour is past, you will be glad to let Lord Elphin go."

"What will you do?"

"I will sing you another song."

"About me?"

"Not about you."

"What is it about then?"

"That is for me to know and for you find out."

"Oh, a riddle! And if I don't guess it, I have to set Elphin free, is that it?"

"You will know the answer by the time it is ended and you will

set Lord Elphin free."

Then Taliesin began to sing again.

Softly he sang, but his voice travelled to the far corners of the hall and beyond the hall and far beyond.

Discover now what I am!
I am the creature from before
  the flood,
Without flesh, without bone,
Without head, without foot ...

Far to the south, the wind that had been busy burying a party of travellers in the desert sand stopped to listen.

I am neither older nor younger
  than I was at the beginning ...

In the far north, the Arctic wind wandering among the ice

and snow heard him calling.

I am as wide as the surface of
the Earth ...

On the wide western ocean, ships were left becalmed as the wind hurried away towards the sound.

I neither see, nor can I be seen ...

Fishermen off the eastern shore took down their useless sails, put out their oars and rowed wearily home as the wind abandoned them.

Taliesin sang on, summoning all the winds of the world.

The crowd in the hall could hear it now, the whispering, the rushing, the roaring, coming from all directions at once.

With a crash that shook the

rafters, the four winds met and howled round the castle, searching for a way in, tossing the slates from the roof and sending the guards tumbling from their watchtowers, ringing the bells in the church steeple, until everyone thought this moment or the next must be the one when the whole castle would come tumbling about their ears.

The song ended. The roaring outside died to a murmur as the four winds hurried away, to be about their own business.

In the hall there was silence.

Even Maelgwyn was afraid.

He sent for Elphin, still in his silver chains. Rhun, you remember, had told the guards to throw away the key.

But locks and bolts were nothing to Taliesin, who had called the winds from the far corners of the Earth and sent them home again.

A few words more and Elphin's chains fell from his wrists and ankles.

"No hard feelings?" said Maelgwyn. "Let's be friends. It's a real pleasure, Elphin, to meet an honest man. All these fools and flatterers almost had me believing that my wife was the prettiest, my bards the finest – and what about your horses, eh? I'm sure you've got one that can beat anything in my stable."

"I'm sure I have not," said Elphin.

"Now, now! You're flattering me. I won't have that. You've spent too long at court, that's your trouble."

Elphin was too polite to point out that most of his time at court had been spent in the dungeons.

A horse-race, that's what Maelgwyn had in mind. Between Elphin's horse and the best in Maelgwyn's stable. And a small bet on the result, just to make it interesting.

Maelgwyn's idea of a small bet was enough to make Elphin a beggar for the rest of his life if he lost. But what could he say? He looked towards Taliesin, but Taliesin only shrugged; Maelgwyn was still the King. If a horse-race was what he wanted ...

"We're going home tomorrow," said Olwen. "We've a long ride ahead of us."

"Let's make it early in the morning, then," smiled Maelgwyn. "Before breakfast. First light!"

"First light would be good," nodded Taliesin.

* * *

Elphin had agreed to race against the best of the King's horses; he hadn't expected to race against all twenty-four of them. But there they were when he arrived at the starting post just before dawn, all lined up and ready to go.

"I couldn't decide which was the best," Maelgwyn smirked. "Not at such short notice. Besides,

twenty-four is my lucky number."

"Elphin's too," smiled Taliesin, smothering a yawn. He'd been up all night, getting things ready.

Elphin took his place at the end of the line of horses. As the sky grew lighter he was surprised to see, a few paces beyond the starting line, another line set out. In front of each of the King's horses a small sprig of blackened holly was stuck in the ground.

It's an odd thing about horses. A horse is a noble animal. An intelligent animal. But he doesn't always see too well. Sometimes he'll try to jump over a shadow, thinking it's a fence. Now the light of the rising sun cast such a long shadow from the holly sprigs that it looked to the King's horses like a solid wall.

The signal was given for "off" and off went Elphin.

Some of the King's horses stood, heads down like mules and wouldn't budge. Some of them backed away. Some of them turned and galloped off in the wrong direction. What none of them was going to do was try and jump that solid wall of holly – tall as a house, it looked!

Elphin galloped on. He wondered vaguely why no one had overtaken him yet, but he was too busy holding on to look behind. Once the horse stumbled and Elphin lost his hat, but he clung on. He turned the far

marker and started back.

And saw what was happening at the starting line. Horses bucking and turning, tipping their riders off, over their heads, over their tails. Horses waltzing round and round as their riders tried to set them at a jump that wasn't there.

Elphin wasn't a man to tire out his horse for nothing. He came back at a gentle trot and crossed the finishing line – the winner!

Amid all the cheering and back-slapping and handing over of Elphin's winnings that followed; "You dropped your hat," said Taliesin. He stared back down the course of the race-that-never-was, to where Elphin's hat still lay, its feather gently waving in the morning breeze.

"Could you lend us a spade, please, Maelgwyn?" said Taliesin.

"Fetch them a spade," sighed Maelgwyn. Then stalked off without bothering to ask what they wanted it for.

Taliesin handed the spade to Elphin.

"Where your hat is – that's the spot where you must dig," he told him.

"How long do I dig for?"

"Until it's time to stop."

Elphin didn't argue. He hadn't been digging long when he uncovered a great crock filled to the brim with gold pieces.

"A small thank you," said Taliesin, "for looking after me

while I was growing up."

"You're not leaving us?" cried Olwen.

"I only promised to stay with you till I was grown. As all children do."

"How shall I manage without you?" asked Elphin. "Giving judgement – advice to the farmers and the merchants – I can't do it on my own."

"You're not stupid, Elphin. All you have to do is look, listen and think before you speak."

"Where will you go?"

"Hither and yon. East of the sun and west of the moon."

"But you will come back and visit us sometimes?"

"Close your eyes and think of

me and I'll be there," said Taliesin ...

In birdsong at daybreak
In the smell of sweet grass after
*   spring showers*
In moonglow
In seafoam ...

So Taliesin left them and went on his way singing and long after he was out of sight the song came echoing back:

For a while yet my fate is to be
Taliesin, but my true home is
somewhere among the stars.

About the Author

Maggie Pearson has had several jobs – from being a barmaid to an au pair to a journalist – but she now writes books full-time. Her first novel, *Owl Light*, was shortlisted for the W.H. Smith Mind-boggling Books Award, and her latest, *Shadow of the Beast* was longlisted for the Carnegie Medal. She has written across many genres – including two historical novels, *The Eyes of Doctor Dee* and *A Slip in Time* (both A & C Black) – but retelling traditional stories is what she most enjoys.

Maggie has three grown-up sons and lives with her husband in a sixteenth-century cottage in Suffolk, and sometimes in the Pyrenees in France.

Other White Wolves titles you might enjoy ...

The Path of Finn McCool
retold by Sally Prue

Giant Finn McCool discovers that the biggest head doesn't always hold the biggest brain. When he annoys the little people, they warn him of an even bigger giant across the sea in Scotland. Finn's big mistake is setting out to find him ...

The Barber's Clever Wife
by Narinder Dhami

Many years ago, there lived a lazy barber who kept losing customers by cutting them and not their hair! Luckily, he had a clever wife with cunning plans to earn the couple money. But was she smart enough to fool the thieves?

White Wolves